Maine Coon Cats

BY NANCY FURSTINGER

The Child's World®

Published in the United States of America by The Child's World®
1980 Lookout Drive • Mankato, MN 56003-1705
800-599-READ • www.childsworld.com

Acknowledgments
The Child's World®: Mary Berendes, Publishing Director
Red Line Editorial: Editorial direction
The Design Lab: Design
Amnet: Production
Design elements: iStockphoto; Shutterstock Images;
Willem Havenaar/Shutterstock Images

Photographs ©: iStockphoto, cover, 1, 12, 23; Shutterstock
Images, cover, 1, 7, 11; Willem Havenaar/Shutterstock Images,
cover, 1; Minerva Studio/Shutterstock Images, 4; Public Domain, 9;
eZeePics Studio/iStockphoto, 15; Warner Bros. Pictures/Album/
SuperStock, 17; Joyce Vincent/Shutterstock Images, 18; Simone
van den Berg/Shutterstock Images, 21

ISBN 9781626873827
LCCN 2014930624

Printed in the United States of America
Mankato, MN
July, 2014
PA02226

ABOUT THE AUTHOR

Nancy Furstinger has been speaking up for animals since she learned to talk. She is the author of nearly 100 books, including many on her favorite topic: animals! She shares her home with big dogs and house rabbits.

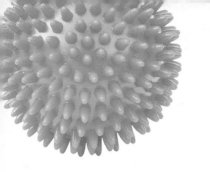

CONTENTS

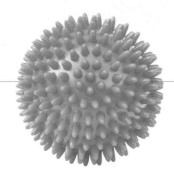

Tame Wild Cats

The Maine coon cat is one of the most popular cat **breeds** in the United States. It is easy to see why! This smart animal is very calm. It also has fun being silly. Maine cats make perfect pets for owners that enjoy playing.

The Maine coon cat has a powerful appearance. It has an all-weather coat. This means it can survive in cold and warm weather. Our country's **native** cat has a thick coat that pushes off water. It has a long, bushy tail like a raccoon! It is native to the United States since it was first bred here. Maine cats are good hunters. They use their teeth and claws to hunt **prey**.

There are about 600 million house cats around the world. Cats in the United States belong to one of 42 different breeds. The Maine coon cat is one of these breeds.

Maine coon cats enjoy being around children. But kids must understand this breed doesn't like to be held. Maine cats would rather follow you around.

Maine coon cats are a smart and popular breed.

Many Tales

There are many stories about Maine coon cats. The truth is, no one knows for sure how the Maine coon cat came to be. It is known these cats were named after the state of Maine. This is where they were first found. Maine cats were also named for their ringed tails.

A Maine coon's tail looks like a bushy raccoon's tail. Maine cats have **tufts** of hair on the tips of their ears. Their ears look like bobcat ears. This started stories. People made up stories about how the Maine coon was created. Some said raccoons bred with wild cats. Other people said bobcats bred with wild cats. Neither of these stories is true.

Another story has a tie to France. The queen of France planned to escape to America in the 1790s. Six of her royal Angora cats sailed with her. These cats have long, silky fur. The cats arrived in America but the queen never did. Her cats bred with native cats to create the Maine coon breed.

Many people believe the Maine coon breed started with ship cats. These cats sailed to America on ships. The cats hunted **rodents** that

snuck aboard. Some cats strayed when the ships stopped in America. They bred with the cats in New England. This new breed of cat could survive rough winters. This is because of their warm coats. This breed became the Maine coon. This is probably the true story of Maine cats.

Maine coon cats have special features that make them easy to identify.

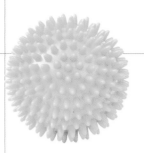

America's Breed

Maine coon cats grabbed interest during the first professional cat shows. More Maine coon cats appeared across the Northeast. Twelve Maine cats entered a Boston cat show in 1878. Maine cats started appearing in other cat shows. A brown **tabby** named Cosey won the National Cat Show in New York in 1895.

The fame of Maine coon cats was short lived. Other longhaired cats from Europe became popular. Soon people wanted the more eye-catching Persian and Angora cats.

The United States' first longhair cat nearly disappeared. A small group of breeders saved the Maine coon. They put on more cat shows. They also displayed photos to call attention to this breed. The breed was officially recognized in 1980. Maine coon cats also became the state cat of Maine in 1985.

Maine cats are one of two cat breeds native to the United States. The other breed is the American shorthair. The Maine coon is one of the most popular cats in the United States. Only the Persian cat is more popular.

Cosey was the first winner of the National Cat Show in 1895.

A brown tabby named King Max won the Boston cat show three years in a row. His son Donald won in 1900.

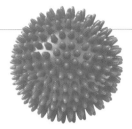

Big and Powerful

Maine coon cats are one of the largest breeds. Males can weigh between 13 and 18 pounds (6 and 8 kg). Females are smaller. They weigh between 9 and 13 pounds (4 and 6 kg). Maine cats may take three to five years to reach their full size.

Maine cats are built for cold weather. Their thick coats push off water. The fur is longer on the cat's back and legs. Their tails are bushy. Maine coon cats use their tails as scarves in the winter. Maine cats have big paws. The paws have tufts of fur between the toes. Their paws act as snowshoes!

Maine cats have long coats. The coats are thick in the winter. This saves the cats from cold weather. The coats thin out in the summer. Their fur is soft and silky.

Some Maine coon cat owners call their cat's ears "lynx tips." The wild lynx and bobcats are known for tufts of fur on the tips of their ears.

These cats have long, rectangle-shaped bodies. Their jaws are shaped like squares. This helps them grip **prey**. Maine coon cats have big muscles. They are strong cats.

Maine cats are built for the cold weather and snow.

Tabby Patterns

Maine cats come in more than 60 different colors and patterns. They can be one solid color, such as black. Or they may be two colors, such as red and silver.

Main coon cats can be one of three tabby patterns. Classic tabby coloring is the most well known. Bold, black markings stand out on the fur. A big letter *M* marks the forehead. This pattern has a striped tail. The mackerel tabby has curved stripes on the side of the body. The patched tabby has patches of cream in the fur.

Maine cats can have different eye colors. Most have gold or green eyes. Cats with pure white coats can have blue eyes. Or they might be odd-eyed. This means each eye is a different color.

A single litter of Maine coon kittens can be different colors.

Although it is rare, some Maine coon cats are odd-eyed.

Gentle Giants

Maine cats are called "the dogs of the cat world." These gentle giants enjoy human playmates! They act like playful kittens their whole lives. Maine cats get along with dogs and children.

This breed loves being a family cat. Maine cats hang out wherever there is action. They are calm cats. But they can also act silly. Maine cats want to be best buddies.

Maine cats are not afraid of water like some cat breeds. They play with the water in their bowls. They even stand in their bowls. They try to turn on water faucets. Maine cats jump into empty bathtubs. They may even curl up in the tub for a catnap!

Maine cats have tiny voices for their size. They meow and purr like most cats. But they also make strange sounds. They chirp and tweet. These noises are the same sounds raccoons make!

Maine cats can squeeze into strange shapes. They curl up tight in cozy corners.

Maine cats enjoy playing with water. You may even find them in your bathroom sink!

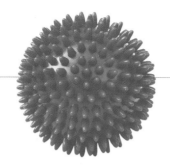

Famous Felines

Most people know about the *Harry Potter* series. These books were made into movies. A Maine coon cat plays the role of Mrs. Norris in the movies. She belongs to the character Argus Filch. Mrs. Norris catches Hogwarts students who are breaking rules. If the students see Mrs. Norris's eyes, they know they are in trouble!

Three different cats played Mrs. Norris in the movies. These movie star cats needed to look messy. They wore collars with fake fur attached.

The Maine coon cat also breaks other records. One Maine cat became famous as the world's longest domestic cat. Stewie measured 48.5 inches (123 cm) from his nose to the tip of his tail. Stewie passed away in 2013 at the age of eight.

Another Maine coon cat became famous for its whiskers. Missi has the longest cat whiskers in the world. They stretch 7.5 inches (19 cm) long.

Argus Filch holds Mrs. Norris after she caught
students roaming the hallways.

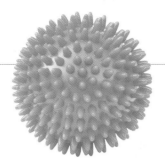

Cat Care

Maine cats are mostly healthy cats. They can live up to 12 to 15 years. Cats need to visit the **veterinarian**. This helps keep them healthy. Vets check the cats and give them **vaccines**.

Maine coon cats are indoor cats. This is the safest spot for them to live. They need beds to take catnaps. Maine cats also need crates for trips. You will want bowls for food and water. Cats need litter boxes, too.

Scratching posts are a good activity for cats. They quickly learn to sharpen their claws on posts. This keeps them from ruining furniture and carpet. It is important to trim their nails sometimes.

Maine cats should be groomed often. They do some grooming on their own. Their rough tongues act as combs. Owners need to brush Maine cats twice a week. Their long coats can **mat**. Burrs cling to their coats. They also shed in warm weather.

Maine cats will groom themselves, but it is still important to brush them often.

Cat Games

Maine coon cats like to bat toys across the floor. Then they run after them. They catch them with their big paws. They might drop their toys in their water dishes. Some cats will even play fetch!

This breed likes toys. They enjoy balls that bounce. They like toys that make sounds. Squeaky mice are a big hit. They also like toys that dangle from fishing poles. They will even play with paper bags.

Some Maine cats play a strange game with people. They jump up so they are head level with the person. Then they will bump against the person's chin or forehead! Maine cats also use this greeting when they are sitting on someone's lap.

This breed also likes to play games of chase. Maine cats will race around. Then they will hide. Two cats make this game more fun. Two Maine coon cats would keep each other company. They would live a long and happy life together.

Maine cats keep busy by playing with toys.

Glossary

breeds (BREEDS) Breeds are groups of animals that are different from related members of its species. The Maine Coon is one of the most popular cat breeds.

lynx (LINGKS) A lynx is a North American wild cat. Maine coon cats have ears that look like lynx ears.

mat (MAT) To mat is to become a tangled mess. Maine coon cat fur can mat if it is not groomed.

native (NAY-tiv) Native is belonging to a place by birth. Maine coon cats and American shorthairs are the only two native cats in our country.

prey (PRAY) Prey is an animal hunted by another animal for food. Cats use their strong teeth to catch prey.

rodents (ROHD-uhnts) Rodents are small mammals that have sharp front teeth used for gnawing. Mice and rats belong to the rodent family.

tabby (TAB-ee) A tabby is a cat with a striped or spotted coat. A tabby may have markings that look like a necklace or bracelets.

tufts (TUHFTS) Tufts are small clusters of hair. Maine coon cats have furry tufts on the tips of their ears.

vaccines (vak-SEENs) Vaccines are shots that prevent animals or humans from getting an illness or disease. Cats should get vaccines to keep them healthy.

veterinarian (vet-ur-uh-NER-ee-uhn) A veterinarian is a doctor who treats animals. It is important to take your cats to the veterinarian.

To Learn More

BOOKS

White, Nancy. *Maine Coons: Super Big*. Mankato, MN: Bearport, 2011.

Zobel, Derek. *Caring for your Cat*. Minneapolis: Bellwether, 2011.

WEB SITES

Visit our Web site for links about Maine coon cats:
www.childsworld.com/links

Note to Parents, Teachers, and Librarians: We routinely verify our Web links to make sure they are safe and active sites. So encourage your readers to check them out!

23

Index